T0105737

EASTERN FREEZER

MIREYA ROBLES

Translated by Susan Griffin in
collaboration with the author

Order this book online at www.trafford.com
or email orders@trafford.com

Most Trafford titles are also available at major online book retailers.

Printed in Victoria, BC, Canada.

ISBN: 978-1-4269-2421-7 (Soft)

*We at Trafford believe that it is the responsibility of us all, as both individuals
and corporations, to make choices that are environmentally and socially sound.
You, in turn, are supporting this responsible conduct each time you purchase a
Trafford book, or make use of our publishing services. To find out how you are
helping, please visit www.trafford.com/responsiblepublishing.html*

*Our mission is to efficiently provide the world's finest, most comprehensive
book publishing service, enabling every author to experience success.
To find out how to publish your book, your way, and have it available
worldwide, visit us online at www.trafford.com*

Trafford rev. 01/18/2010

North America & international
toll-free: 1 888 232 4444 (USA & Canada)
phone: 250 383 6864 ♦ fax: 812 355 4082

CONTENTS

EASTERN FREEZER

I leant back in my seat and tried to track these quick flows of consciousness that crossed my brain of plastic tubes, without timidity, but with an almost ethereal lightness. I know that I died in 1973 when they were going to manufacture vegetable meat in Chile. I know that I died in 1973 when the latest news flash informed me that there was a flaw in Skylab. I was reborn yesterday and forty eight hours later -now days have forty eight hours- I have yet to emerge from my surprise at being alive. The year 2273, a double leap year, a year in which we have two Februaries. "Two thousand, two hundred and seventy three". The numbers sound different. People choke as they speak. The strange sound of a bone rolling around and hitting against an empty, desolate, sloping passageway clatters in their windpipes. Speculation: the air has thickened and now sounds like hard cement. Speculation: the air has become solid. Speculation: their respiratory system has changed and they grind the air. Speculation: they aren't suffocating, they have changed the way they breathe. Speculation: my respiratory apparatus, no, not apparatus, my respiratory system is inadequate for the purpose of breathing air. Speculation: they're regulating my respiration.

My gaze skips quickly from one place to the next: I do not stare at my feet. Skip-skip-skip-skip. No, I am not connected in any way to anything outside myself. Speculation: remote control: no. No. No. No. Speculation: I am independent, I walk, I tire; I walk, I recover; I walk, I am surprised. On my own. For

1

myself. For. Speculation: in myself. Speculation: modern lung. Speculation: in me. Speculation: alien to this world. No: in it. But not in control of myself.

There is no cold in the air. A fine heat. Breath. Steam. A dry steam. A contradiction, but I do not perspire. "We interrupt this programme to bring you an important announcement: Skylab... We interrupt... Skylab... the announcement... the telephone number is 343-1111... no... in that one they give the time and the temperature... Skylab... the announcement... the telephone number is 869- and the other numbers... who dials the number... my mouth does not move... this grunt is not my voice... the Skylab... this programme... heavy... heavy... dial the number... Sky... di... the num..."

Yesterday at exactly ten o'clock they told me that I had been alive for about three hours but that one always took some time to regain consciousness. I thought... No. I heard without thinking. I remembered nothing. I headed towards the door where they gave me absolution. No, that's not the word: where they discharged me. And my rehabilitation? And my training? And my possible traumas? Quickly, while she took my papers from the file: "Psychology no longer exists. The words are still the same. There are many new words, but the old ones, those ones mean the same things". No. Not philology. And that course of *rapidus-rápido-rabdo-raudo*. And isn't *raudo* the most vulgar word because it evolved more than *rápido*? No. The course: a waste. The course: obsolete. "Language does not change because the means of diffusion kept us all speaking the same across distances and time. New words: there are those". She didn't even say this to me as if it were serious information. Only as a way to occupy herself with something before reaching the counter from the filing cabinet to have me sign a certificate of invalidation of death and an authorization of the validity of my birth certificate. "You are reintegrant 47111. A metal badge. But it's better to tattoo the number onto yourself. On the sole of your foot: 47111. Your brain is new. It <u>should</u> work well. But one way of not worrying is

2

to take precautions: reintegrant 47111. We do not force anyone. Everyone knows what has to be done. The law is precaution and precaution is the law. The tattoo machine: in Hall Eleven on the second floor. Automatic machines. The ink is black. No, blue. No, dark. Blue-black. Enter the number 47111. Five seconds. Yes, you can walk immediately afterwards. Oh, sign the register. Year 2273. Reintegrant 47111. No, no letter. Just 47111. Yes, everyone will know. There is only one reintegrant with that number. No. There is no over-population. No. There are no more births. Everyone is a reintegrant. The world population is now at 47111. Not inhabitants, reintegrants. The others: they're all in freezers. You came from the Eastern Freezer three days ago. Yes, in our transporters. Now you can pull the loading sticker off the palm of your hand. I never give so many explanations. Go to Hall Eleven on the second floor. No, there is no identification paper. Just the number of your reintegration. Yes, tattooed. I never give so many explanations".

For some reason the idea of returning to the Eastern Freezer and never going to Hall Eleven on the second floor seemed attractive to me. Yes, my reintegration number was pretty: 47111. Immediately I feel attached to something: my number and I, me and my number, my number in me. I am legs-sweater-skirt-sports shoes-key ring-sunglasses in a complete and absolute 47111. This encourages me to walk. The key ring, a round medallion: Sagittarius. The colours of a stained glass window: Sagittarius. Two green keys: Sagittarius. An aluminium key: Sagittarius. A chain: Sagittarius. And me a complete and absolute 47111.

The process of marking me was so quick-cold-impersonal that it reminded me of that other life. When everything was becoming mechanized and one already felt mechanized. A white curtain: I pulled it. It was of canvas. Above: metal hoops. I closed it for a useless privacy: there was no-one on that floor. That Thursday -it ought to be Thursday, I want it to be Thursday- I was the only reintegrant. Posters, directions. Black letters, white boards. REMOVE YOUR LEFT SHOE. I took off my right shoe: 47111

3

should not be wasted on a left foot. I raised my leg until it was perpendicular to my body. I inserted my naked foot into the foot-shaped opening of the machine. It looked like one of those machines they called an "artificial lung". A cold touch on my foot that had the power to surprise me. I liked it. A quick stinging, precise and scientific. Speculation: this is a Chinese thing with their acupuncture. I have always liked Chinese acupuncture. The idea of painlessness. The dull and deadened noise stopped. I seated myself to look at the sole of my foot like the statue of the boy looking at the thorn.

I leant back in my seat and tried to track these quick flows of consciousness that crossed my brain of plastic tubes. Uncle Sam's tavern: call it a memory; the Rip van Winkle area; the chubby statue of Emma Willard: the triangular area, the Tri-City area. At one end, Mario's restaurant: "Salad with roquefort cheese, shrimp a la Newburgh, black coffee, sherry from Jerez. Stout beer, if you have it". The masks, red hued. The masks with their frozen grimaces; the corners of their mouths fixed upwards. Petrified pain: it doesn't cry either. A cut. Empty... empty... empty. Disconnection. The thread breaks. A blink. A strain. An almost ethereal lightness. I am... I am in... I have no names... The streets are called... Everything is blank... "It should work well... it's new... it should work well... should..."

The same frustration as in those mechanical times: 11174. Everything continued being so precise: the left foot was not the right foot. The neon sign, of red light, began drawing, intermittently, in black: CANCELLED. REINTEGRAL CANCELLED. CANCELLED. REINTEGRAL CANCELLED. A small ticket appeared like the ones that were vomited out: measures-weights=scales... scales... scale rather than weight... and let there be the word and there was the word: scale... and they told you your weight and your fortune. "INSERT YOUR RIGHT FOOT TO CANCEL THE REINTEGRAL. AT THE END OF THE TONE, WAIT TWENTY SECONDS. INSERT YOUR LEFT FOOT TO RECORD THE CORRECT REINTEGRAL." It also seemed like a cooking recipe, with all those verbs of command. That old joke about "putting one's foot in it" tasted bitter. Because all this went much deeper and was more serious, to the fact that there was no way to choose. And now, there is no longer anyone to rebel against. Absolute automation. Absence. Steam. Cold steam. Cold. No-one. Nothing. Not even me. And the 47111 imprinted, placed -not given-, placed precisely in the centre of the sole of my left foot. A 47111 that is not mine, that determines my belonging to others, to another thing that I must search for. There is a certain apathy within me and a slow urgency to know what world it is that I am being born into.

I leant back in my seat and tried to track these quick flows of consciousness that crossed my brain of plastic tubes. I had only been alive for about forty eight hours. On my foot: no strange sensation. As if the number did not exist. The Chinese: acupuncture - acupuncturists. Painlessness. A cold anaesthetic. My number and my foot in my shoe. I walked along one of the desolate hospital corridors. I shrugged my shoulders about three times, what to do, resign oneself. But resignation is troublesome. One gets tired very quickly. One gets tired of always returning to the same thing. One gets tired of being automated. And if I were myself, me-individual being-unique-myself? Worse. Or perhaps not. The ME of myself and not in anyone. The ME of myself and not for anyone else. Even more depressing: for nothing. Now, a toy-rabbit-guinea pig trapped in a laboratory. They take me back and forth. And always, how alone. I stand before the counter. I was carried there by those shoes I once wore in Greece, in all the temples. On all the sand. On the counter: a bell. I rang it several times. I see the same filing cabinets: there they discharged me. The nurse isn't here. Something tells me that it is useless calling her. You don't belong to yourself, but you are alone in this emptiness. That's what it is: empty. Empty. Empty. A vacuum. The woman wore a hat that I translated as <u>helmet</u>. It was better to call that thing a helmet. Engraved. Metallic. With fleur-de-lis engraved on it. Old, curly, bleached hair. No, not old, old fashioned, like in the thirties. Like the years 1930 onwards. What she was wearing was, definitely, a uniform. I would say her helmet and her jacket were Roman. The jacket: not metallic, but a mouse-grey colour. The colour mouse-grey. With many large scales. No, peacock eyes. Or scales. And her skirt: straight, austere, down to her knees. Leather, high heeled, black shoes. And all of her indifferent. Made. Not born. Not from inorganic stones. Like the vegetable meat in Chile. Walking through the polished-corridor-desert in my shoes from Greece: "Like Chile's vegetable meat. Vegetable. Like meat. Vegetable. Vegetable. Like".

Empty corridors. Rolling stairs. No, rolling ramps. Without stairs. A monotonous movement. There are no noises. There is an absence of noise. Absence. Absence. A lower level. A ramp. Another lower level. Moving. A passageway painted on the floor, or a long carpet, flowing up to the doorway. It opens automatically. I must leave. I had to leave. I leave. I left. I stop. A park. Streets. Everything deserted. A plastic world. Made from plastic materials. I don't know if the consistency of objects is like rubber. It seems to have been made by Dalí. I look for those warped watches. I wouldn't be surprised if everything were to be transformed into a desert of sand and if the warped watches were to appear there. There are several cement hedges in the park. Everything solidly constructed, compact. Nothing vegetable, nothing alive. There are various labyrinth-like corridors that lead to various doors. All closed. It can't be: the process must continue, I am not in the freezer, they've only just released me. A rectangle, a darkness, an open door. I no longer think in order to make decisions, I take them, I start walking. Darkness. The tunnel. Not a prisoner. There was an exit. I move forward. As if the floor were moving. There is no fear. I move forward. Darkness. The tunnel. It will lead somewhere. Soon. Very soon. It will lead somewhere. Darkness. Thickness. Light. They pushed me. I was pushed. I came out. A small vestibule. Tiny enclosures, like the changerooms in shops. In the third one on the right, a number: 47111. I entered. There was my uniform. The same colour. The scales-eyes of the peacock-mouse-grey. But there was no helmet. I was glad. Speculation: I'm not a public employee. A short, pleated skirt, and some open sandals that I want to call Roman. Dressed in all that. Disguise-uniform: my new skin. Again: a feeling of belonging. I am my number, perhaps not my number, but my uniform. New instructions: I can keep my sun glasses and the bag I always carried over my shoulder... hanging... with those long straps... the bag... black leather... down to the level of my hand. I began carrying it as always, hanging from my shoulder down to my hip and I touched it with my hand as if it were a weapon, a machine gun, my protection. In my bag, the key ring. I quickly took it out, it was mine, it was me. The green keys and the aluminium one. The stained glass of the key ring holder shone oddly in that strange sun. But not the letters: they always read Sagittarius.

I started asking myself what kisses would be like. I started asking myself what bodily functions would be like. I felt plant-like and I recalled the anguish I used to feel when I inhabited my last skin: I was human and all the life that surrounded me was vegetable. No human starved because of me, for me. And the need to give myself to someone was spread amongst the dusty cracks of the bookshelves. I continued walking and arrived, undoubtedly, at the city centre. Men with full length leather aprons. Movements made by animated dolls. Guiseppe, the shoemaker from *Pinocchio*. You could choose any of them. They all looked alike. They were all the same. Craftsmen. Like dolls. As if their craftsmanship were a way to wind themselves up in order to continue. The slow movement, the skill. The women: buns at the nape of their necks. Full-length aprons. Baskets. Assistants: assisting the craftsmen. It failed. That business of liberating women ended up failing. But no: there are no supremacies here. It's a question of measuring physical strength: to each the work they are capable of. They do not look at one another. No one looks at anyone else. Nobody would care that Socrates died by poison. Nobody asks himself if he brushed his teeth before taking the hemlock, nor what kind of toothbrush he used. A.D., B.C., letters, only letters. There are no births. No sex. No passions. I know this because of myself, there is no going back. Vegetable, everything is vegetable. Nothing is being lost, it has been lost. And to think that in California they had started to defend Safo. And one had been proud to declare: "I am". But all that was a challenge. A revolution. A challenge to the inquisitional bonfire. It was a struggle that extended to other states and to other cities but I only know what happened in California. And a poetess wrote poems to another woman: *to a handsome woman*. And all this was a challenge. And it was a struggle. And they were drops of water in the gigantic flame of the bonfire. Useless. All useless. Everything is unisex. No: asexual. Mechanized, vegetablised.

Speculation: a multiple memory must exist. An intimate one: mine. Like my keys. Another, common to all of humanity. Speculation: I have retained a little of each. This section of the city: craftsmanship. The next: giant bookcases placed in parking lots, on both sides of the street. All the book covers are of mother-of-pearl. No: they're plastic. I opened one: there were no letters. Buttons. Only buttons. And next to each button, the reference: June, 1973. I pushed the button. Successive, quick, news flashes appeared on the screen, which I immediately identified as the last ones from my time. I shut the book. I wanted to know no more. I continued on my way.

The next section: administration. All the buildings were capitol buildings. There were ten. "Legislative Capitol". I entered. A vestibule. Another. Long, polished, interminable corridors. Door. Corridor. Opening on to another door. The great legislative hall. Blind. Everyone is blind. They don't wear uniforms. They had all lined up. In neverending lines waiting for their turn to sit down. I arrived a little before the session began. I chose what I considered to be the best seat. I leant back in my seat and tried to track these quick flows of consciousness that crossed my brain of plastic tubes. I had been wandering this world for the past forty eight hours. The blind people lined up guided by their dogs, supported by their walking sticks. In the front part of the hall, a small table bearing a microphone. To the right, a large table like a banquet table, where the legislators used to sit in the old days. A little above eye level, there were portraits of each of the legislators. A little higher. Eye level. A uniformed reintegrant guided the first blind person. He touched the microphone and began caressing the letters in braille as if he were playing the piano. His complaint was drawn out, profound, echoing. A long beard. A stick. A cloudy and revolving gaze. Immense, sunken eyes. Patricio. It occurred to me to call him "the patriarch". Patricio, the patriarch. The name suited him perfectly. His proposition: "It is unfair that the effort to manufacture artificial eyes has been abandoned. The manufacturing of the other organs has been perfected. Their honours, the legislators, know that it is no longer a question of counting on transplants. Organ donation ended when the era of the reintegrants began and only us blind people have been left incomplete. Those that brought with them their natural eyes can perpetuate them. And us?" He stood up slowly. I admired the wisdom of his walk and the dignity with which he leant on his stick. Patricio, Patricio the Patriarch. A blind woman with an unfocused and revolving gaze followed him. Always caressing her braille. Intelligent. Brilliant. A legislative mind. I would hand over to her a blank constitution so that she could write it. Civil rights. But above all, do they not even know this? HUMAN RIGHTS. The third: a university professor. Blind. Blind. Blind. He laughed at the stupidity of man. He remembered how, in the last third of the twentieth century, no waiter wanted to serve him a drink to "save his responsibility". Blind. He was blind-blind. And he laughed at all the waiters. He had faith that the reintegrants would be more intelligent. Civil rights. But above all, do they not even know this? HUMAN RIGHTS.

A bell rang which declared the session closed. From each portrait. From the bottom portion of each portrait a long parchment appeared. The spokesperson collected them and placed them on the banquet table. Uniformed. Monotonous voice. He began to translate: promises without foundation. Speculation:

this had not changed. Indifference. The blind people. They filed out. Dignified in their handicap. I could not resist the temptation to shake Patricio's hand. I promised to tape for him some of my verses. He told me that he had been in Chile once.

I descended the marble stairway alone. Desolate streets. I noticed then that there were no restaurants nor food stores. Neither was I hungry. Nor thirsty. I proceeded up the street. The entrance to a subway. As I drew near the grille opened. A ticket. Strange, yellow lights. Everything deserted. Speculation: there has to be an industrial section where they manufacture the mouse-grey material. Speculation: I'm a thinking being. Just that: thinking. Those strange, yellow lights. The locomotive arrived. A black, iron ghost. The seat isn't bad and there is no-one to bother you. Speculation: this must take me to the Eastern Freezer. That's not bad, to go to the Eastern Freezer. The train stops. I get off. Speculation: if there are cars maybe they are "Model T" cars. I have always liked "Model T's". The station: a capsule. No, it's not the Eastern Freezer. A huge sign: STORAGE AREA. I step onto the red carpet: the machine spits out a ticket: "Reintegrant 47111. Niche 72. Storage hours: Thursday, 20:45 to Friday 8:45. Friday: Exit B, 8:45. Destination: Craft Section". Evidently they don't make long term plans here. Evidently, it's day-by-day. Some naturalist would call this a "beehive". But all the urns were made of granite. It was easy for me to find niche 72. It was easy for me to accept the existence of all those urns occupied by immobile reintergrants. It was easy for me to accept that these were not the tombs of Charles V nor of Phillip II. I stretched myself out in my urn which I found cold and protective. At my feet: my purse-bag of black leather. The keys. It was not important that these keys have no use: they remained mine. With quiet surprise I recognised in myself the old capacity for sleep. I could still sleep, that was all that mattered. We always have <u>something</u>. This encouraged me to settle myself. We always have something: the key ring. A round medallion: Sagittarius. An aluminium key: Sagittarius. A chain: Sagittarius. And me a complete and absolute 47111.

THE PARADE

The man had the exact girth of Sidney Greenstreet and the softness of Peter Lorre. But he lacked the cynicism, and the surprise in his eyes. He was lying back, in all his fatty monumentality, on a folding chair placed in the front part of the orchestra section, which was uncovered, leaving behind him the rest of the empty stalls, clearly organized in an amphitheater with a cement floor. The man distractedly dug the edge of the sole of his right shoe in the mud which comprised that strip of earth. He was alone, abandoned, and he glanced at the nails on his hand from time to time, without having any reason for doing so. He knew that someone had taken him there and he waited without impatience, without resignation, without hope. He allowed his gaze to wander in the darkness of the night. He was wearing a suit of white drill, a fine, linen shirt. He was soaked in a perspiration that cooled in the caress of that strange breeze. His wide forehead, touched by something that had a humbling effect. Perhaps by the fact that he had been dragged to that place despite himself. Despite the fact that he knew that it was all useless. The light, yellowish, a light sienna colour, began to slide, licking a rectangle in the space that stretched before him. Fantastic lights, drowsy in old colours, violated the earth to form a stage. From the left emerged, like a bitter and sad mouthful, all the characters that made up the parade. They were touched by that same, strange light and they moved forward dancing the Charleston, joined in an indefinable and far-off rhythm. Those women in their silk dresses with their long, infinitely long waists. With a band around their foreheads. Curly hair, stuck to their scalps. The men, with straw hats. Characters from all the silent movies that had been shown on all the screens until 1928, the year in which, irrevocably, they awaited death.

The man collected the sweat from his forehead with his cupped hand. Automatically, slowly, he drew his handkerchief from the pocket of his trousers, a handkerchief made black by the filth, wrinkled by the weight of his keys and a few coins that he fingered in the rounded material of the pocket. He carried the handkerchief to his forehead, several times. And he felt himself fall into a type of stupor. As if everything had ceased. As if everything had stopped. His bladder felt full and he wanted to urinate. He reconstructed before him, from his imagination, that passage that lead from his bedroom to the bathroom and which he followed several times during the night, when he awoke sweating, his eyes fixed on the ceiling, motionless, until he convinced himself to take one leg from the bed, the other leg, to sit up, to stand up. And to think, while walking down the passage, why does one have to wake up and feel like death. How is it possible that one can walk heavily, dragging oneself through the night, drowning oneself in the emptiness, when everything inside is dead. While he listened to the jet, he was amazed at the miracle of urinating. Of functioning mechanically, dragging in one's feet, the heavy bulk of his body.

The fantastic characters continued populating the illuminated rectangle. From his seat, the man wanted to stretch out his hand, so as to reach, so as to join himself to that odd form of life that paraded before him. But he remained motionless, sweating, like a fatty animal. You could almost say that he identified every gesture made by these beings: the blink of the eyes lined with charcoal, bordered by deep, grey circles under the eyes. Their movements were quick, like the convulsions caused by the accelerated projection of the celluloid. But there were other gestures reserved for the expression of deep emotions, that were performed slowly, in a drawn out manner, stopping at each point of their intensity.

The white suit made the large sweat stains at the joins under his arms obvious, in the cloth arms, in the drill ribs. The man felt his intolerable heaviness, as if his body denied him movement. A moment that he couldn't quite identify had arrived. In his large eyes like those of a sick animal, something began to bother him. A cauterization. As if they were burning the very centre of his gaze. A light. Wires made of light. Wires that formed a figure. The figure of a man. An electric man. The same man that had brought him to this inexplicable place. He stared at him, with a slow curiosity bordering on idiocy. The ethereal and luminous character began drawing an expression of painful anguish. An expression of anguish that was independent of that large and immobile being but which, at the same time, belonged to him. And more and more he began feeling that there was something in that being that was, sadly, his. As if it were his own energy projected before him, inviting him to participate in that parade that was destined to disappear with the brevity that sows for us pockets of death. That was it. Perhaps it was about that: about taking from him the death that he had collected inside himself. Of convincing him that a loss has to be followed, of necessity, by a compensation. A compensation. One must live. One must live to await this. Of convincing him that everything is balanced.

The fantastic and luminous being pointed out to him, as if they were places one finds and points to in a map, the perfect balance in the characters in the parade who advanced with brusque, quick movements, like puppets, but at the same time projecting the intensity of their passions. An intensity that saved them from being puppets. The luminous being opened his hands like a fan, separating his fingers made of dry, incandescent twigs. Suddenly, the anguish of his gesture intensified and he broadcast an echo: "Salvation is the balance between the automation that imprisons us and that secret life called pain".

The large man, deformed by obesity, had understood. He had understood long before hearing the words of that electric lightening bolt humanized by anguish. Of course, he had understood, but he was unable to feel anything. He was unable to react. Autism. Autist. The curse. A curse on himself. Without being saved. That luminous man: failed. The pain of that failure could be felt in the air. Could be felt in the atmosphere. The large man: autistic. Without the bones to move himself. Made vegetable. He lowered his eyes a little like Sidney Greenstreet. Lacking in cynicism, he began wrapping his hands around himself like a chastised child. And a light, like the one in his room, like the one in that passage down which he dragged himself at night, soon fell, taking over the desolate space that surrounded him.

MY HEART GOES OUT TO THE BLACKS OF HARLEM

We're robots, destined to devour ourselves in the veins of our solitude. The fence grows. We raise it to the song of psalms of love. We put walls around space and space and space until we have walled ourselves in. And in the meanwhile, we sing psalms of surrender. We asphyxiate ourselves in the empty space carefully constructed without windows. The lack of light and air feeds us with death. And we sing psalms of surrender. We're in an igloo permeated by absence. Bricks, bricks like a hollow beehive over our heads. The capsule that we build with our teeth anchored to earth, blocking the way for others. Our pockets, filled with sweets to deceive ourselves. We take out one: "I love humanity". We take out another: "I love the vets wounded in Vietnam". We take out another: "My heart goes out to the Blacks of Harlem". We have met our obligations. Now we can go to other lands. To the Costera Criolla bus station and stand there as if we were stupefied, letting our gaze play over the many busses that await departure like docile animals. We go South. During the night we count the sandwiches and coffees consumed by the bus driver. We allow the radio to invade the atmosphere with sweet boleros. Our foreheads are pecked at by crows. Belgrano, Palermo, the Torre de los Ingleses, Libertador Avenue. And those transparent and deep eyes beating on our backs. Beating me on the back.

Everything is deserted in Mar del Plata: the casino, the monument dedicated to Alfonsina Storni. And behind the monument, something that breaks our surprise like a slap: "Storni Hotel and Restaurant: Drink Coca-Cola".

I return. Costera Criolla bus station. Exit. And suddenly, I'm in Florida and Lavalle Streets.

We-I-he decided to leave the igloo. To participate. To make possible Sturgeon's dream: to be the first human of the future, composed of other beings. "Read Sturgeon. You must read Sturgeon". The words resonated in his ears like the echo of a guru. To participate. To join with others. To unite with one human being. To break the capsule. To pulverise the igloo. The igloo imported from North America, USA, and to tear it to shreds on Mayo Avenue.

The atoms have been disintegrated. The capsule pulverised. Free. The city of lights. Free. He walked in the night's humid air. Belgrano, Palermo, the Torre de los Ingleses. Libertador Avenue. District Eleven. To stretch oneself towards the cutting edge of the blade in search of the guru. To go and meet him. To break the night's rebelliousness.

Disconcerted. The guru. A capsule. The guru in a capsule after the manner of and similar to his. Like that capsule of his that had been pulverised on Mayo Avenue. The guru's capsule: with no windows. To knock. To hurt your knuckles. To feel the dull swelling of your joints. Calling. Shouting at the windowless walls. Silence. Isolation. He circled the capsule with a progressively uncertain step. A sign. Black letters clearly painted on the white wood. Like those they use for "Don't walk on the grass". He didn't want to read them. Words were not enough for him. He had come determined to confront the Master's deep and transparent gaze. To tell him that he could join with him, that he could be part of him, that he had broken solitude's barriers. He circled the capsule with an uncertain step, until the light of dawn began drawing, with all its transparency, the desolate body of the houses, impassive in the face of the swarming vehicles. Involuntarily, he stopped before the sign and read, as if in a language he didn't understand: "Read Sturgeon".

The return. Braniff. Flight 901. Kennedy Airport. The same walk through customs. The same faces in immigration. A trip without incident. Baggage claim. An old woman with arteriosclerosis, insisting that she had just arrived at Ezeiza Airport, shouting in a loud voice that they bring her a bus to take her to Belgrano.

Exiting the airport. He caught a bus that took him to his town. He was surprised by the passage of the months spent seated in his room, meditating. Everything was not lost. He was free. He had to use that freedom to change the direction of his existence poisoned by isolation. If the doors to <u>one</u> human being were closed to him, why not dedicate himself to a race? One race. The suffering race. The Blacks. The Blacks of Harlem. He underwent a period of dizzy and recurring trips to the heart of Manhattan. He stayed in the Sheraton Hotel. In the Hilton. Saw all the Broadway shows: "Fiddler on the Roof", "Cabaret", "Applause". Walked until exhaustion down Fifth Avenue. And, as the weekend drew to a close, returned to his town taking Madison Avenue which leads to the freeway. And, upon entering Harlem, locked all the car doors, closed all the windows, so as not to be infected by that sub-humanity. And, upon examining his conscience, told himself that he had not been so bad to the Blacks. That he once invited some Africans to his house whom he allowed to eat off the very plates of his dinner service. He had also criticised the undignified roles played by Blacks in the Hollywood movies. He had also shouted a few times that Blacks should not have to sit at the back of the buses. And they ought to allow them into the restrooms in all the restaurants in the South. And that was enough. He continued walking down Fifth Avenue for his love of the Blacks. In the Hilton: for his love of the Blacks. On Broadway: for his love of the Blacks.

During one of the many returns to his town, he took a detour to Mount Kisco. He travelled roads unfamiliar to him.

Lunch time: he looked for a restaurant. He entered William Street hardly looking at his surroundings. He parked his car comfortably in a wide space next to the sidewalk. He walked a few blocks and began to notice that he was in a small Harlem: a black neighborhood. He quickly retraced his steps until he once again felt safe in the privacy of his car. He travelled the streets until he found a high-class cafe in a white neighborhood. He slowly approached the door. Before entering, he rested his gaze on the figure of an old Black man who was cleaning the garden, rhythmically collecting the dry leaves. Almost in unison they exchanged a "Good morning" with a nod of the head. With his spirit lightened, he entered the air conditioned comfort, satisfied with his magnanimity. Unaware of the solitude that enveloped him like repeated circles of an arctic cold.

OLD FRANK

He lived in a place in the West and everyone who knew him called him Old Frank. He was only a story, an unimportant legend. He lived, without knowing it, in a world that did not exist. He had erased the lines from the map. It was of little importance to locate his solitary figure on some exact point. All that mattered was that he insisted that he lived in the Nevada desert. As an involuntary recluse. Carried there by his last gesture of renunciation. The last town he had visited, now many years ago, was Las Vegas. Not to lose himself, like the others. Only to convince himself that evasion was impossible. He observed the human cargo at the roulette tables, in the frenzy of the slot machines that pursued him like implacable tormentors: in the gaming houses, in the pharmacies, in the hotels. He had crossed the luminous panorama of the Strip with its false gaiety, with its false lights. The exact place and central bank where the essential values were negotiated in dollars and cents in exchange for false laughter, phantasmagoric and grotesque in the unbearable heat of the night. He remained part of that orbit for a few days. Allowing himself to be lead like a broken doll. Until one day when he emptied his pockets, leaving the last cent he carried on the sidewalk and walked off. He had no idea where his steps would lead him. He found himself, soon, on the highway. From time to time, some traveller offered him the comfort of his car and he went, with his gaze fixed on the speed, without saying a word. He had lost all notion of time. As if waking from a dream,

19

he became aware of the driver of the pickup truck. He tried to say something to him, but the words that he thought did not find their voice. Suddenly he made out something that seemed far away to him, a type of cabin, the remains of a ghost town. With a gesture he communicated his intention to get down. With a vacant stare. A slow step. He walked towards the cabin. The entrance consisted of a frame with no door.

No-one noticed his existence. Although bit by bit he was transformed into an unimportant legend. Visited by travelling salesmen who tried to sell him tractors, cosmetics, insurance, lots in the cemetery, cars of the latest model. And they were a little surprised by his silence that they were often unable to notice. From time to time some traveller arrived to ask for water. And they got used to the idea that he was there, as if waiting for them. Old Frank and his dog, Mickey. No-one knew what they found to live off and, at times, to get off the subject of the temperature, they commented that Frank was a very mysterious man, who lived off roots, or who went for days without eating, like Kafka's Hunger Artist.

Frank lived through their stories and one could say that he invented his own history. It was enough to have met her and then to retain her presence through the years. Everything occurred in that strange city. An encounter that should not have marked the direction his life took. That transparent and deep gaze. Her breath like that of a healthy animal. To talk to her while looking at her mouth, to have followed closely the conformation of her smile. To feel himself touched by the magic.

Everything ends. Everything inexorably ends. As if everything beautiful always awaits the death sentence. But the speed with which situations change is disconcerting. The irrepairabilty of failed meetings is disconcerting.

He had lived the years of his youth without recording dates. He had not recorded his birth, nor the death of all the sons he did not have. But this was much more than a date. It was a moment that became Friday, the twenty seventh of July. He was fulfilling one of those social obligations as one does, so uselessly. He found himself surrounded by beings and comments to which he was indifferent. He needed to call her to calm the tension that was beginning to strangle him. He said something about an important call and he moved away from those ridiculous and conceited beings for a few moments:

"I only wanted to tell you that I miss you".

"Where are you?"

"With friends. But there's something missing. Here. In the atmosphere".

No other words were necessary. The last that they said to one another, although later they spoke often.

Saturday. A dark and gloomy atmosphere: *Beowolf, Hamlet*. As if to provide the setting for a failed meeting. Painfully insignificant causes. Empty hands. All he was left with was the search. The search which would never cease to mark his step. To look for her knowing that he would never find her. To look for her to the point of absurdity: to leave her to greedily conserve shared moments. To see her so as to feel from close up her absence. To convince himself that it is all useless in the face of what is irreparable. Until one day when he left forever. And he continued looking for her far away, very far away. In other voices that were not hers.

Old Frank, with his overalls, and Mickey, lying at his side, with his large black spots. They did not need to communicate. They understood one another. At two thirty Old Frank left the cabin with a happy look in his eye. Mickey watched him leave, without moving. It was the time when Frank needed to be alone. To look for her in that desert's empty kilometres. To return serene with a peace that transcended, that went beyond his astral body. Every day he eliminated ground where he would no longer have to look for her. Without realising that the desert was all the same and lacked markings. He would spend the rest of the day wrapped up in himself, in his solitude. At nightfall he would sit on his porch with his shotgun at his side and he would remain with his gaze fixed on the vastness of the desert, waiting for her.

Mar del Plata
August, '73

THE DEATH OF THE TIGER

"Save the tiger," Jack Lemon would still be shouting when he went to collect his Oscar. Save the tiger. This was once heard on celluloid. Signatures were collected to save the tiger. Everything went very quickly. A question of seconds. More than anything, to follow the fashion of "conservation". Nature must be conserved. Another beautiful mission for the Boy Scouts. But the tiger is already dead and there is nothing we can do in this reality that is no longer violently sad. The tiger doesn't carry his death upon his back. He carries his absence. How useless to congregate on Sunset Strip to pretend to witness death as if it were a show. They have changed the names. Something as basic as the lexicon has undergone a transformation. And everything so naturally. As if an army of words had swallowed arsenic to delay the effect and to conceal a violent death. The tiger walked slowly. With steps that were far from obeying his will. He did not know if the death of his intestines had anything to do with the death of the words. He was sure that he had not swallowed arsenic. That the last liquid that he had swallowed came from a bottle of port. With very clear letters that he had understood very well and which went under the label: "G & D", bottled in the San Joaquín valley and, as if to provide an intimate note to the beautiful label, below the words "Tawny Port", they had written: "Private Stock". He also knew that the soul of that being that had taken possession of his tiger skin, had left it. And he could even arrive at the exact moment: in Chinatown in Los Angeles. And if he made a small effort, his memory would tell him that perhaps it was not far from the sidewalk where the most celebrated Hollywood stars imprinted their footprints with the weight of their bodies. Of course, this possession would seem somewhat suspicious today, a case for exorcism. He never revealed to anyone the mystery of this possession. He transmitted to no-one the strange monologues conducted by that soul that would be called "lost", but which actually sometimes spoke with a certain serenity. It would be more correct to say that he did not speak, but rather felt out loud. Or better yet, that he transmitted without speaking. Always the same obsession, always the same hoarse shout invoking the past. W.C.Fields, Mae West, Chaplin, Garbo, Tallulah. Who did not return, and why wouldn't they return? Sometimes his precision was embarrassing: that in 1974, at five in the afternoon, one twentieth of April, on the Merritt Parkway, also known as Highway 15, running north-south of the state of Connecticut, he had an urge to masturbate. That he had thought in the solitude of the highway with some grief, that perhaps it would be for the best to die during masturbation at the moment when all the other cars became blurred and the sign that indicated every so often the number 15, always repeating North-South, would cease to be important. That was what he knew of that soul that had possessed him. The beautiful moment of a solitude-death-masturbation. His obsession with W.C.Fields. And then, that escape along the prints of the Hollywood stars: something that had emptied him, like an intestinal discharge.

He knew that his skin was striped. He knew that he was slowly walking along the Strip. He also knew that, upon approaching the word cemetery, his own death would take place. He smiled and his smile felt a little cold. They wanted to save him. That was something to laugh about. Nobody can save someone who has been condemned to death. And he thought that deep down they knew that. They had watched him plant the signs in the garden of words. He remembered how carefully he had written these words on the sign which he thought was the most beautiful: LOVE-

FRIENDSHIP. His pace became slower. He entered the cemetery through the opening in the grille. And, as if it came from other voices, he said to himself: "The tiger has returned". The tiger has returned. The tiger always returns. The eternal return. As if he had to die in a particular spot. On his favourite sign he saw the first words change. They had been crossed out with stripes of paint that seemed obscene to him. Under what remained of love-friendship, they had written: imposition-tyranny. He became even more aware that he was not able to save himself. Everyone was dying of loneliness. But when he had tried to plant something as simple as love-friendship, they had considered this a tyrannical intrusion, an unacceptable imposition. In this world in which everyone has forgotten the art of acceptance, of receiving, it's vital to transform oneself into yet another monolith with legs and arms and mechanical movements. All of this was very clearly laid out in the Statutes on Human Rights, appropriately sealed in an envelope with blue stripes. And when he read them, he recognised the exact moment of his death and the way in which it would occur.

He continued onward in this soft earth, rich in minerals, that offered a strange contrast to death. He stretched a little, experiencing a sensual pleasure upon recognising the last movements of his striped skin. He gave up his attempt to make out the other signs. He did not even feel enough curiosity to see what changes the other words had undergone before they died. The two most important ones had died. That was enough. They were, furthermore, registered in the statutes as something venereal, like a contagious disease that no-one wanted to catch. He slowly rested his head on his front paws stretched in that soil that could be fertile. And he smiled once more when the last cold invaded his skin.

CREME DE MENTHE
AND SODA

The passengers arrive in the train that never arrives. The passengers that are not and exist arrive. The passenger who is there but does not exist arrives. Solitary paths. Solitary rails. Dry heat. An atmosphere in which one feels the emptiness. Everyone ahead. Her, behind. They speak about hats which are characteristic of some place. Cheap table linen in Lisbon. Or better still, Cascais. The guide chants a Te Deum and her heart falls with boredom. If he would only shut up. If they would all only shut up. Now she has almost managed to shut out the sound of their voices. The driver, with the sad look of a bull that is going to charge with its intimate poverty, presses down heavily on the accelerator. The vehicle is a coach. But isn't it absurd not to call it a train? Trains are the only mode of transportation for destinations without direction. Where are we headed? In the coach, to Cascais. Why are we travelling? In train...

A fat body, chubby, in the shape of a overblown football. A man made ancient by years of exhaustion. He drags his espadrilles. You can see the odour of urine on him, although someone said that he is a clean old man and, in fact, drawing nearer to him, he doesn't stink. The eyes of a cow with a slit throat. The heaviness of a disemboweled ox. A reddish-violet face with cheeks like plump buttocks. They say --because he doesn't speak-- that he came here to spy. She doesn't consider his spying to be important.

She reduces his function to zero. She imagines him falling from the fifth floor... if he were to fall from a fifth floor he would utter a gruff roar in Catalan and upon falling to the ground he would oscillate like a pendulum in his roundness before returning to a vertical position, head up, untouched, and would again begin walking heavily in his espadrilles.

The sisters. Dry. Inviolate. Virgins. Forever virgins. A nasal, masticated way of speaking with their false teeth indicating a Spanish from Cataluña. They're made of straw, of wicker, of desiccated age. They have children. The travellers say that they were never legally married. Contradiction. They must have been magic conceptions, remote. While asleep, someone must have thrown down, next to their bodies incapable of nudity, some infants that they thought they had given birth to. When they say "my child" the word sounds like an obstruction in their dusty grimaces.

Another two sisters who make us think of huge Virginia hams. Blonde hams, wearing glasses. Hams with two feet and two arms. They speak solidly in Catalan and she doesn't understand. But, even if she were to understand, it would matter little because they say nothing. Firm voices that do not communicate. Hams surprisingly capable of fat, fleshy smiles. Hams stuffed with Portuguese shawls, with Portuguese table linen. Happy transporters of souvenirs destined to rest in some old cupboard in Barcelona.

Cascais becomes interesting. She walks, I walk, in an isolation that almost hurts. Facing the sea. The hams, the two dry old sticks, the roundabout-inflated-football, the driver, and the guide, mischievously effeminate, feverish, madly effeminate, are spilt through the different stores in Cascais. They're all tourists. They're all still savouring the emotion of having shaken their Highnesses' hands in the Estoril. They were also taken with a type of pink pelican and a monkey that were there. The fateful train-coach has disappeared. Now there are boats, colourful boats, the sea breeze and the humid rocks. And that taste of wood in one's mouth. I can still touch that moment with my hands. Before me are the boats and the breeze. That moment is still close. Solitude is outlined, moving out towards the horizon. That moment is still there. That moment in Madrid in which, between Crème de Menthe and soda the child-virgin cancelled me as a human being. All because I told her my truth. I awakened her longings for raw meat. Cannibals. They're all cannibals in this race of gods in which we create others in our image and likeness. The child-virgin, desiccated in her thirty six years, handed over to me, while she sipped a trembling cup of tea, my banishment papers.

The next day, while I boarded the train-coach, headed for Lisbon, it seemed to me that my luggage was a bundle of dusty bags. That same grey dust from the road, dry despite the rain, that filled my lungs. But no, it was all a nightmare. You don't die simply because others condemn you to death. The girl-virgin was a straw judge. Desiccated in her memories of the Civil War. I imagine that the Civil War must have been very annoying to her, like a buzzing bee that she waved away from her skin with a bony slap. But the child-virgin was no executioner. There are the boats. In some part of Cascais the effeminate guide is trying on, perhaps in secret, some woman's sandals. And the hams are consuming table clothes. And the spy, urine soaked and fat. And the driver, with his cow eyes. There are the boats. The air's humidity. The waves breaking between the rocks. Everything is there, everything must be there, although I can no longer see it. No, the child-virgin is a straw judge, but she's not an executioner. The waves fell silent. I am shaked by a huge wave of nausea. My lungs disinflated and I spilt myself in a hemorrhage of liquid wood.

Cascais

ANNIE

His right shoe touched the third step. A muffled noise. The second step. The first. And there it was: the path. The atmosphere was clear. The narrow earth path tightly trodden, invited one to walk it. On either side, thick trees, with their tumultuous load of placid leaves, almost doughy with their green flesh. A quick glance at the sky. Only to convince himself that it was still there, like a painted theatre curtain, which could be reached by rapidly crossing the air's transparency. Breathing. He breathed. Above all, he was exactly aware of the moment in which he exhaled. He stopped, not to measure the path, rather to confirm once more the idea that it was there, waiting for him. He had reflected a long time after finishing the last page of *Anna Kleiber*. In some mysterious way, Anna Kleiber had become a voice, circulating blood, happiness drowned in sadness, mystery and evident reality, hope devoured by pessimism. But even stranger still, Anna Kleiber, just like that, emerged from the letters, as a being who did not project herself into the future, towards <u>her</u> future. She was a small being, a shadow reduced by the distance of time, persistent and sad, who moved further away without disappearing. He knew that Anna Kleiber was at some point in his life. It was a question of setting out to find her. Beneath his feet he felt the solidity of the foot path. He left behind his house made of old boards. Of clean boards, as if they had no heavy conscience. Piling up without rigid force to form that house, at a distance from all the others. A house that could be <u>seen</u> to rest in amongst nature.

His repeated steps began to be felt in the swelling of his feet. Little by little the sensation of security that had sent him off on this search faded. He began to feel confused, helpless. He was unable to hold on to his initial feeling of purposefulness. It was an incoherent or, at least, imprecise reality. Involuntarily, with the toe of his shoe, he made a pebble jump and fly forward. He followed its trajectory with his eyes. He felt it beat the ground and allow itself to fall, resting on the earth. Slowly he raised his gaze and began making out a small house, poor, clean, whose piled boards reminded him of his own house. He did not believe in symbols. He did not believe that the pebble could be interpreted as a North Star which led him to his small self, to his child self. He stopped in front of the house. He felt his right foot falling on the first step. The second. The floor of the front porch. That house was not unknown to him. That house was waiting for him. He stood in front of the door and waited. He did not have to knock. An old Black woman, with white hair tied in small plaits that crossed her head, opened the door. Her attitude was calm. It was not necessary to exchange greetings.

"I was waiting for you."

"And Annie?"

"You're late. It must be so bad for you to know that you're late?"

"And Annie? Who is Annie?"

"Annie has always lived at your side. Since you were born."

He began, I began to remember that this old woman sold tickets in that village where I was born. I recognised her manner of dress. Clean. Her long dress. The lottery tickets. And Annie playing on the ground, at Jacks. Annie, always Annie. And always, her preferences. I remembered for a moment the explanation that they gave me: I was satisfied with anything. This was what our aunts specified repeatedly. First it was necessary to buy things for Annie because I was easy to satisfy. I was never able to make them understand that not shouting at the top of my voice did not indicate consent. But we continued to recognise that we were brother and sister. Perhaps because our aunts reminded us of this with that bit about "Brothers and sisters should be inseparable". Moreover, the stricken faces of those lunatics obsessed with honour united us in secret rebellion against them. Especially when they shouted in fury: "You have sullied this family's honour". After this we knew that they would punish us by locking us up for a week. But I was never able to understand whether this restored their honour to them. Perhaps because they never told me what this honour was nor how we had sullied it. Then we took refuge in the studio and we let the days pass quickly by playing innumerable games of Canasta, which, almost always, Annie won. Also, sometimes we laughed remembering the furious faces of those old women mourning their honour. The obsessive rigidity of these crazy women became progressively more asphyxiating. They insisted that Annie had to become more polished so as to behave as a lady, as a real lady, should she, one day, be invited to a banquet. We never understood why banquets were so important nor why one had to live in preparation for them. I only remember that Annie, each time she heard them, behaved in a more vulgar and grotesque way.

Coffee made with hot milk and bread. That's what we had for breakfast. Annie said to me: "Any day now I'm going to get married. With any foreigner who will take me away from these witches". Two weeks later Annie left our town forever, with her husband. At the time she was eighteen years old. Throughout the wedding the witches cried because "it was indecent to marry a foreigner who was not even rich nor aristocratic". Annie attended her own wedding as if it were someone else's. And when we embraced, we cried. Not because of the emotion of the occasion but because, suddenly, we felt, heartbreakingly, our approaching separation. A separation which would be definitive.

We heard from Annie frequently during the first six years of her exemplary marriage. After that her letters became less regular until we ceased to receive any. Someone informed us of a violent change. Of Annie's trips to the most lowly and depressing bars. She drew away from her children, her husband. She left the house for days at a time. She spent time on the docks obsessed with merchant ships, with sailors. She allowed herself to be carried by the bitter happiness of believing herself to be more woman, more beautiful because of this. Any bed, any bar, any man.

I had always intuited that uncontrollable force which dragged her towards her own death, and I felt myself to be too much on the sidelines to try to stop her. I tried to ignore it, to forget, to forget her.

The old woman left the door wide open, but I did not enter.

"And Annie? Is she dead?"

"No. She's at the María la Grande's Bar, about three kilometers from here."

She did not have to say anything else. It would not have been necessary for her to tell me that Annie was not a shadow of her old self, and that everyone said that any day "she would take a handful of pills".

I returned along the same path, slightly damp because of the evening air. My house seemed very welcoming to me, and my old chair where I usually read seemed comfortable. Distractedly I touched --my hand resting on the table-- the shape of that book. *Anna Kleiber.* I focused for a few moments, on the book, on the title. Until I decided to place it once again in the empty space that it had left in the bookcase. Why should I feel such profound peace? What gave me the right to feel such profound peace? Perhaps the certainty of knowing that it was impossible for me to prevent her death. Perhaps the hope of intuiting the moment of her death and the thought that she would die feeling my affection. Or perhaps, because that afternoon I had regained Annie. And obsessively, her image as a small child came to me, playing Jacks, with her pink dress, on that floor with its arab mosaics.

THE PUDDLE

In line, Laurita is once again in line, six years old, with her child's eyes like cups of coffee, her mouth plump and soft; before her and behind, white uniforms and school shoes; already that warmth has started, that incontainable pleasure: every day at the same time, in line, in front of everyone else, the liquid wetting her small slit to continue in its downwards path, slithering between thighs pressed tight until soaking her socks, her shoes, until it forms a puddle of yellowish transparency on the pavement; now to take a few steps forward, or back, to change her position in the line so that the Big Ones will be misled when they investigate the puddle; but they already know her story and the nun's enormous hand lifts her small, plump hand; and always the fright of seeing the nun approach with rapid, long strides, the air lifting her veil pregnant with prayers and the large hand and the small hand, in upward-downward nervous movements; and always the same, but child, why have you wet yourself again, right now, to the bathroom, wash yourself, and I'm going to tell your mother, but child, why do you have to wet yourself everyday; and the nun's complaint, and I already know that the nun is going to lodge her complaint and at home I will find the bricks that my mother warms so that I can sit on them because the doctor told her this, that I'm cold somewhere inside, and I sit quietly on the warmed bricks because that's what my mom told me to do; and the next day I'm on my way to school, clutching my books, and the classes and break time and the games and the classes and time to go and time to line up and I think I'm going to wet myself; and the nun comes to watch me, Laurita, I'm watching you; but the warm liquid is already snaking its way through the small slit, past her tightly pressed thighs, her socks, her shoes, until it forms a puddle on the pavement.

GRAND CENTRAL

A poem is written in prose. On the walls, on the carpet. The letters fall in the empty apartment and, in a premeditated carelessness, they become longer and flexible, visible voices, the open vowels of your name. Your name... your name... your name... And the tiredness in my voice dreams of actually touching you. It dreams, it dreams, the dream, I dream. Your hand stuck to the window and the sound of the engine that separated me from you. Grand Central. The movement of the train. The cold and mysterious night. The platform grew distant. And your steps... and your steps... You will take the underground, the subway, and at forty second, the shuttle, the shuttle-train in the bowels of the earth. Exit-Salida, the stairs, the cold air of the street, you will breathe in mouthfuls of shadow. Your gaze a little sad, will search out your final station, Port Authority. Your bus-coach, westward. The tunnel, your town. My train continued hooting in the night. Hudson Line, looking for the northern towns. The neon lights were too bright for the nostalgia in my eyes. Next to me, a rancid, antiquated little woman, looking as if she had suddenly sprung out of an old trunk. She gave off a disturbing smell of moth balls. A faded beret, a feather in the beret. Protuberant teeth. A dimple at the corner of her mouth. She smiled frequently and her smile made lines around her eyes, as if she had been up to some mischief. She said that there were a lot of people on the train and I said, yes, that there were a lot. She said that she worked just across the street from Grand Central. That it was easy to take the train: you just had to cross the street. That she could take the 6:20 train but that she took the one at 8:30 because her work was so interesting that she couldn't leave it. That she became so absorbed and that she got so devoted to her work that she literally found it impossible to leave it. And I asked what her work consisted of and she said that she did the books and that the numbers transported her. That it was difficult to put aside the numbers but that she was also a poet. That a poet should write clearly and without complications, like the epic poem fifty pages long that she wrote about a canary and his mate that had several baby canaries. And how the canary and his mate taught the baby canaries to fly and the baby canaries flew from the cage. To live their life. And that the publishing house to whom she had sent the epic poem said that they were not interested in ornithology. And that she sent it to a society that was interested in birds and they told her that they were not interested in poetry. And this was why the poem hadn't been published. And I asked if she wrote love poems and she said ten in honour of her deceased husband. It seemed strange to me to hear that one could write poems in honour of somebody and it seemed impossible to me that love could have penetrated that dry flesh. And she said, that in addition to the ten poems to her dead husband, she had written fifty poems to a suitor she had had for four years but whom she hadn't been seeing for a year now. And I measure the dryness of her flesh and the deep lines on her face, that hide that reluctantly covered her bones and it was impossible for me to associate that tragi-comic-old-piece of junk with love. And I said that I was also a poet and that I wrote strange narratives and she said, that she knew that my narratives were oneiric and she showed me her teeth --dimple at the corner of her mouth-spark-smile in the corner of her eyes-- and I said that only some were oneiric and she said that she had hundreds of poems and they had published some in a magazine that she used to edit years ago, for the Association of Weavers and that some members of the association congratulated her on her poems, but others didn't. And that she did not have a university degree because who needed one. And I said that I needed one despite my allergy to university degrees. And she said that it is the fault of the bureaucracy and I said yes. And she said that she had attended the Medical School for three years but that she did not continue because who needs a degree: they could keep it. But that yes, she did work for some months in a hospital with patients who suffered from mental problems and I asked if she was an analyst and she said no, that she taught them to weave wicker baskets and I asked why she left it and she said that the patients loved her and that they wanted to learn to weave but it was all the bureaucracy's fault. And I asked what the bureaucracy had done to her and she said that above all the nurses and that now she was fine with numbers and that she only had to cross the street. And that it had been a great joy finding me on the train, that one never knows. But she had to get off at Riverdale. And that what was my name and she pronounced it several times and that she was Cecile and she removed a glove and squeezed my hand and she got off before we reached Riverdale.

The Scarborough station was cold and deserted. Upon leaving the train I gazed around me looking for other passengers but no-one else had left the train. I recognised my car parked in the parking lot and when I got into it I experienced a strange feeling of emptiness. The desolation that I had left behind, in Grand Central, came to mind. In that café-bar. The yellow light in our faces. The lamp open over me, like a flower. And my smile, bitter. That tasteless meat, that aromaless tea. The salad opening superfluous leaves, like wax. As if none of it were capable of undergoing the normal function of being digested. In my temples, a hammering pain, squeezing me, gripping my thoughts. On the other side of the table, your presence is diluted in anticipation of our separation. It was the moment in which looks and voices ceased to produce communication. It is useless to try out words that insist on turning themselves towards the exhaustion of empty plates. The smile which goes no further than a mechanical gesture is useless. I wanted to be different for you. I wanted to create a private corner where you would not be able to intuit my transformation, the sombre expression that accompanies me in your absence. The closed face, the tenacious hammering in my temples, the aborted smile. I should have undergone all of that on my own, in the same savage privacy in which an animal voids its intestines. I was a little embarrassed by this anticipated transformation which took place before you, when I returned to the first decade of this century and I slipped away in the flesh-plaster of a metaphysic painting.

In my apartment, silence awaited me. The white, iron table, forming leaves in the air, simple, as if built into a frieze. On the glass, the two candlesticks. The dinner. That dinner. And in your eyes, the golden light of the candles. Blue tunic. And your beauty, touched by magic. I became serene thinking that, on that night, I had been able to pass on to you a happiness that you had never felt before. And that, perhaps, this would serve as compensation, as a balance, for this death that I had given you tonight. I wanted to shorten time by going to sleep early. In the evening lethargy, your studio-atelier, your Manhattan studio. A horse. His hooves breaking the glass. A rider, your father, you. The horse on its own. And you, floating in space. The floor-precipice opened and the horse fell into the abyss and you, without falling, feeling the bump of your fall, like someone who moves, at great speed, towards the centre of the earth and you continued to float amongst the frames and the horse, in its grave, headless, and the head, with the bit between the teeth, is shown, like a display, amongst the glasses, adorning the window. My eyes are open. Sweat licks at my back. The semi-darkness of my room. And in my hoarse voice, the open vowels of your name.

Three in the afternoon. Five o'clock. Six o'clock. The voice of the TV presenter transmitted reports through metallic vibrations. I asked myself whether they were broadcasting some unimportant announcement: the time and date of some speech by Gerald Ford. Or some heartbreaking piece like the terror caused by the army of worms that marched down the stairs in an apartment building in the Bronx, after invading the rotting flesh of an old man who had been dead for fifteen days. One of the public authorities took responsibility for removing the body, but no-one wanted to be involved in the task of fumigating the apartment. Interviews with and complaints from the Hispanic neighbours: futile. I heard nothing more. I don't know what will become of the worms... "The temperature, 30 degrees fahrenheit. A possibility of snow. Humidity, mist". The 19 inch screen. Important news. The black and white picture. A plastic bodybag. Several police officers. Manhattan. In front of a Chinese laundry. A dismembered body. The head separated from the body. And the members, tied up with a nylon cord. There are no suspects, but there is someone who insists that she is guilty. Before the camera zoomed in, I began making out the faded beret with its feather sticking out, the protuberant smile and the infantile joy at the corner of the eyes. "Cecile, you can call me Cecile". And they continued questioning her with a condescending air.

THE OTHER HALF OF TIME

The woman with the Carthaginian eyes looked out to sea and her gaze extended over many centuries. It was a ritual. A rite. To meet the past in the silent vastness, in the vague murmur of the salty foam. The crisp morning, the silence outlining her silhouette. She knew that she had lived many reincarnations and the past, without files at its fingertips, lacked information. But there she was, with the weight of a millennium's worth of tensions, and the sea. And above all, that feeling of destiny: a place and a date. Like an appointment made before birth. It was a question of transforming daily death into a period of waiting. It was a question of visualising that other being, on the other shore of time's tension, cleaving through air and space, or motionless, overcoming the wounds of a gentle desire running through the veins of her skin to rest in the warmth of her hands. The meeting. It was a question of finding one another. And there, on the other shore, the damp sand seemed to wrap around the atoms of an echo. Resonance, voice: reply. The woman, untouched by common hands that circulate cents and coins, allowed herself to be caressed by the air, by a breeze that penetrated her profound silence. Behind her there remained that house that once, in other centuries, had been inhabited by slaves. Rites of Santería. Possession by spirits that spoke through the mouth of a medium. Choked messages from other eras that persisted in joining with the present. But the North-Star voice that should show her the meeting place never materialised nor allowed itself to be heard among the messages sprouted by those who fell into trances.

Once more facing the sea, open to the suggestions of those echoes that enclosed her past. The waves, like docile workers, deposited, in the slowness of their movements, pieces of wood, ribbons of seaweed, bottle caps, bottles. A bottle. A perfume bottle. The woman's hand picked up the bottle and, clasping it in her soft grasp, she drew it towards her closest silence. Her gaze alighted on the alien glass, on the atomizer, and on that liquid wounded by the rays of the sun, that had the consistency of unction oils. She allowed the scent to touch her skin and she felt then, like she had in other centuries, ready to leave a locale, this time an open area, to begin her search. She placed, with a movement of long habit, the perfume on the skin of sand that served her as a dressing table. She turned her gaze to the wood. Towards that piece of wood lying there, patiently, as if waiting for her. She felt the dampness of the thick plank between her hands and tried to make out the strange letters that formed a message in a language that today was already unknown to her. She noted that the board was meticulously parted in two and she drew to her breast the damp letters, as if to embrace them. Without having a precise awareness of what was happening, she believed she understood. She straightened slowly and with a firm step she conquered the expanse of the beach. In the distance, the station. And in the isolation of the tracks, the solitary trains. A ticket. The conductor with his visored cap. The quick movements of successive images. And over the loudspeaker, the name of a town.

She waited for the train to come to a complete stop. She felt herself descend the steps and suddenly, appear on the platform. The extensive group of passengers dissipated, into the building, carrying with them luggage, greetings, hugs. In the clean space of the platform, the silhouette of a woman. Her gaze, intense, her figure, carved in silence. Motionless. In her hand, half a plank of wood bearing strange letters.

A brief pause. A peace full of longing. A profound and ragged breath. They moved forward to shorten the distance. They looked in one another's eyes, and recognised each other.

THE TRAIN

It is not the right time to explain to myself who these people are, what we are doing here, at the exit to this darkened factory; I don't know what I did inside there, among those boards, rotten grey wood, nor do I know what I did during the day today, I know that I worked with those women, that whole group of women that asphyxiates me a little, I remember the rotten wooden walls and I think that inside there, with those women, I was part of a workshop and that I sewed. And now this determination to leave, here, facing the door to the elevator that never quite arrives to rescue our brusque patience. We continue standing there, I continue standing among the shadows, but they're not shadows because I can see their dresses and coats and their scarves stuck to the head and the shine of their eyes; they don't talk nor do I talk nor do we talk but we can hear the feeling and we know the impatience of waiting; this paper bag where I kept my lunch, now, rolled up between my hands, I don't know why I draw it to me as if to protect it, perhaps it's because some piece of apple still remains in it. We stay there, standing, eternally standing, but I have the freedom to look at the ceiling, and at the dust, and at the corners, and at that spider web; if the spider web were of iron it would almost make the same drawings of the bars in the patio dining room, the bars of that window, the house in that town that now lives outside space, beyond the limits of that region, because in that region, that town that now lives in a corner of my memory has already died; now I know, at last I know, that each time someone in the town dies, the town changes, it stops being to some extent, it is no longer the same without the one who left; I learned this when that old man died, because I had so often said to myself, and what had that man been born for if he was only a parasite, if he hardly ever worked, because Batista didn't give him work and Grau gave him a small position in which he hardly ever did anything and Prío Socarrás gave him another small post in which he hardly did anything either, and I always had to listen to him talking about the rest, so-and-so is a lazy bones, that one, that one has always been a lazy bones; and the other, the other one is a thief that steals a lot at the Customs House; and me looking at him, but how can he talk like that about others, this parasite who has been brought to this world for what? And the day when his death arrived, I learned that he had been born to form part of the town's configuration, because now Crombet Street won't be the same without seeing him walking, dragging his oh-so-long legs a little; his hands, crossed behind him, crushing his linen *guayabera*, and that smile in his blue eyes, of self-satisfaction, of self-condescension; now I see him like that, always doing what he wanted to, never doing anything, and that his arrogance was only a deep weakness; now I also know that all this is unimportant, that the underground animals are removing his flesh to leave his bones clean and what I know profoundly is that it doesn't matter, because he will have found his self-complacence in space and I want to think that he will have found a lit path; but the town is now incomplete because his voice is no longer in the afternoon of that open-air cafe and the noise of his erroneous dogmas no longer echo in the earth's corners.

The bundles are still behind me, wrapped in their rags, dumpy, heavily loaded; but I don't know if they're made of fat or flesh or of some almost matter that I could cross. Now the elevator creaks its way up, the slow movement, the noise of rust, almost dry, that will stop to open its door before me; I have a premonition of the avalanche of bundles pushing forward, rushing to enter, I move forward to cross the mouth of the elevator, I wait, squeezed into a corner for the mass of people to enter, but I wait on my own and the faces are there, before me, without moving, as if they knew; I get in, I see the weight of my right foot sinking through the wooden floor, and as the door closes, I think that the floor is about to give way and when the rotten wood opens, that descending box of an elevator will throw me down into the emptiness inhabited by thick cables; but screaming is useless, and gesturing, and fear.

I don't know what happened to my memory nor why I'm in this train, at this speed, standing, in the outside part of one of the cars; the noise like a monotonous fight and the coupling of this car with the car in front of it, struggling, as if they wanted to get away from one another; the speed decreases as we approach the town's station; further on, a bridge with arms of steel where I know I have to get off although I don't know why; the train doesn't quite stop, how do I let the driver know if the train is empty and now I see that there is no locomotive; it's vital that the train be stopped; I turn, behind me, a lever; I raise my arm, I pull, I pull, the train comes to a dead stop and immediately makes a brusque motion amongst squeals, like the Caimanera train when it starts moving; I throw myself to the grass to save myself from the speed and, from there, almost at once, I manage to see the train out of control, derailed; I hear the sound of the thunder, the crash with the other train heading this way, and the screams of the people: "the bridge, the trains have crashed on the bridge;" I see them run there and all attention is focused on the possibility of there being people wounded. I see the bridge's steel, twisted; the police heading that way with the innocence and the benevolence of the police in movies of the 40's; I try to stop them to inform them, to tell them, I didn't mean to cause all this, but they should know, I pulled the lever; the accident wasn't my doing, I just pulled the lever; the police don't stop to listen to explanations and I decide to say nothing that will connect me to the accident, I retreat a little from the tracks, I move closer to a river of black water that seems to contain the night's darkness, until I discover, it's the blackness of oil; I don't want to enter, I don't want to wade into the river, but fear is useless and I enter; if I only knew what it was I had to look for; the police, from the bank, gesture to me to come out because they have heard my wish when I said to myself, if only these police would come and help me, if only they could show me what it is that I have to look for in the river, but they don't want to divert their attention from the accident and, because of this, they want to evacuate any living form from the black waters. They continue gesturing and I return to the bank with my clothes dry, intact, inexplicably intact; there is something strange about me, now I know what it is, where is the rest of my clothing, my sweater, my jacket, the one you gave me, Chachi, I was wearing it, and in the pocket, my wallet; now it's just this pullover that covers me with its tenuous cotton weave, its short sleeves, its blue letters, "I get off on the West Side". The night's cold has left my body; I must return to the river, that's where my jacket and wallet and money for the subway and the money for the ticket I buy at Grand Central Station are; I wade into the river, in this blackness where fear is useless, I make out my jacket almost within arms reach, I stretch out my arm, and before I touch it, I am surprised by the police who come to evacuate every living form from the river and I return to the bank, dry, as if untouched by the black waters; I search once more in the pockets of my blue jeans and find two pesetas and two reales; the telephone booth, I enter, I want to dial your number and I have forgotten it, I dial three numbers, 453, and then, 5225 and the telephone goes ring, ring and you don't answer because that isn't your number, because I have forgotten your number; if I call the painter, the sculptor from Jackson Heights, I know that she would come, but I can already visualize her studio and the telephone ringing, penetrating the canvases, penetrating the marble of the faces, and her walking through the shadows without hearing it, without hearing me; I replace the receiver without dialing the number, without feeling the fear of loneliness, because fear, now, is useless; my hand remains on the receiver as if awaiting some decision that I can no longer make, until little by little I raise my gaze, I pierce the light of the booth's glass, and I see you there, standing, Chachi, waiting for me; and I am going to tell you, I forgot your telephone number, I need money, Grand Central Station, the ticket, contact the painter, the sculptor, and I am going to tell you so many things more and I don't say them because there you are, looking at me, because you are there, waiting for me, and you know everything.

THE VAMPIRE WHO
GIVES BLOOD

He had no lime in his bones. He had no shape, neither had his skin hardened to form his body. But he had the gift of provoking an optical illusion and every one of the others, with doubts and suspicions, came to see him almost as a man. They didn't accept him, they would never accept him, and their voices became dense, were filled with a filthy solidity, when they said "that man". But there was no time to analyze situations and no-one stopped to make comments. The vampire was a serious, silent child who drew pictures and letters to learn languages. And when his mother didn't know it, and when the others didn't know it, he went to the back room of the restaurant, to the opium den of those Chinamen and he became absorbed in the mystery of the faraway gazes with a small notebook in his hand in which he noted strange monosyllables, his secret treasure. Always one Chinaman of about fifty broke the mystery because he was dressed in the same shirts used by the rest of the town. He gently pushed the small vampire towards the door and repeated with a strange sound the same words: "Tonight, bring your notebook to the front of the restaurant". And something strange happened. The presence of the sullen five year old began painting enigmatic smiles amongst those beings. The small form with the notebook did not know how to smile but he learnt to say monosyllables that provoked a commotion amongst the Chinamen and some dried their hands on their aprons and others stopped washing dishes and others stopped filling glasses of water. They all made comments with an euphoria that surprised him. And immediately, the fifty year old man appeared and then one had to forgive him that, at dusk, the mystery had been broken, because he made the small form feel like an oh-so-important being. He took him to an anteroom and he helped him to climb onto a tall chair so that he could comfortably reach the top of the table and there the form wrote down in his language, the sound of those monosyllables. And in the notebook full of numbers and greetings, was trapped, in the flat stripes of the pages, the world of that being whose innocence did not yet intuit, within himself, the corruption that others did not have. What he did ask himself frequently was what the Chinese woman Simona would say if he greeted her in monosyllables or if he counted from one to five for her. There was no-one quite like the Chinese woman Simona. She was always dressed in a long, blue robe. A cone-shaped hat protected her from the sun. Her gaze was always towards infinity and her gestures, of tiredness and sadness. She had many children, the Chinese woman Simona, but none of them appeared to have come from her. Once, surprisingly, she arrived at the restaurant and spoke slowly and deeply. The small form felt his hands turn to ice and he thought that if the Chinese woman Simona passed that corner, he would count from one to five for her. But he felt like vomiting and he suffered palpitations and opened his eyes very wide, and he remained motionless. Shortly afterwards the moment of the great separation arrived and the notebook was lost forever.

It was always four in the afternoon when that form, bathed and dressed, sat down in the porch facing the street and became thinking matter. Or better yet, meditative. He only meditated. And it was then that he felt some guilt, and some terror and he felt like a being inevitably condemned to punishment. And he only waited for nightfall in order to hug his mother once more, so that she could help him sleep and so that she could tell the others to keep quiet. But the day of the great separation arrived and his mother's hugs would be lost forever. From now on he would wear a uniform and he would carry a school case. The train always left on Sunday afternoon and when his mother reached him, saying goodbye to him, a paper bag of sweets, he asked himself why the sundering was always felt in one's throat. The aunts' big house, the feared austerity, knowing that God exiled from paradise, these were the elements that made up his loneliness. And he began to feel that an unstoppable love that seemed to him to be made of blood, forced him into an abnormal orbit, to a stress that embarrassed and hurt. He smudged papers that he carried to the train especially so that some acquaintance would give them to his mother. But this did not save him from that secret ritual of crying alone. Later on he had to be careful. And more, much more. The oldest aunt found him crying and accused him of having allowed a dishonest violation. And faced with the terror of the stain, of another terrible and new stain, he confessed that love-blood that he felt for his mother. No-one could believe it. Nobody suspected that all his interior machinery was absurd, and all his architecture, pulled out of position. All that was left to him was to write those inkblots and to wait for a reaffirmation in the letter-answer, that it was possible to return to the maternal breast. To the uterus. Inside. To the placenta. To swim, living off another human being. But the central place had to be his, only his. No more children. No-one else. And although he meditated without logic, he was able to realize that the rite could only take place through the letter-answer that would come on that train that passed by the saltworks, by Novaliche, until it reach the station from where you could see the river. And he created an illogical pact, one that could never be kept outside his deformed reality: the complete submission of his love-blood and, in exchange, the possession of the entrails of another being. But the letters-answer became infrequent. Or they were sent to someone else. Or they deviated from the ritual line. And the train from the saltworks and Novaliche arrived at the station at the river to bring sweaty and smelly workers that bought plantain chips when they got onto the platform. And a strange sensation began invading that vampire who believed he derived nutrition from the entrails of another human being. And he began asking himself if that blood, his love-blood, wasn't invisible. And something, like broken glass, began falling, towards the bottom of his arteries, in his interior time. The great separation arrived, and the letters disappeared.

The journey to the capital was made slowly, with that luxurious Samsonite suitcase. He had read only a few lines, written with spider's feet, from someone who was looking for students for a guest house. That letter cast the die. It attracted. Also, it asked for <u>decent</u> people of <u>good moral values</u>. And it was interesting not to know whether he fell into that category. The taxi left him at the tip of Aramburu Street. He asked for her immediately. And waited timidly in the sitting room. A woman with a disagreeable appearance, like those that appear in the circus for being excessively overweight, told him to wait. She did not dare tell that desolate being that she had not yet arrived. She would be there tomorrow, first thing. He walked up the street, up to the steps of the university. The Law bar seemed noisy and strange to him. And those guava pies, like a useless attempt to switch off loneliness. He did not know her yet and already he had prepared his blood for complete submission. For all the tenderness that he was capable of. For all the love. And once bloodless, to feed off her. He wandered through the streets, waited for the morning in an exhausting vigil. Early, very early, she arrived. Her frank smile, her beautiful face. How did she know to choose those exact words? "You will see how well you feel here". The pact was made. The love-blood entered her and he heard her say repeatedly that "he filled her soul". They devoured each other mutually. She gave herself over to the task of purifying him, she pulled off his prior skin with her teeth and gave him back his innocence, suckling him like a deer. But nothing escapes the inexorable law. Death, distance, separation. And everything was lost forever.

Exile. God exiled. Cain. To the east of paradise. In the law of evolution, a link missing. Carrying his punishment knowingly.

And the disgust of others, within reach of his hand. Containing himself, contained. But thick blood overflows. And everything wounds. Because any word carries the old accusation of oneself. And then one feels the uncertainty of the clumsy person who looks for truths he cannot see. Who looks for hands he doesn't know how to seize. Imbalance. Dislocation. Only in that city was he able to discern something in the giant signs, in those monumental letters: "You smear everything". "You always break that which is beautiful". And, while he searched for some roses that he thought he carried in his hands, he shrugged his shoulders in the mysterious cold of the night and he felt something freeze inside, as if it were lacquer and varnish.

Buenos Aires
July, 1973

THE FLOATING CITY

Suddenly, the darkness of the night, the fading light, the train station, yes, some train is waiting for me to take me to the city that I knew, that I lived, the city with wooden houses, with small white planks; the switchman with a lantern in his hand, balancing in a pendulum the carbide light, climbs onto the platform and shakes his head with its visored cap to contradict me, no, it doesn't enter here, this isn't your train; I insist, the movement of the visor reaffirms, no, this isn't your train, and the gap in the night hardens like a closed door; I have to leave, my backpack over my shoulder, I walk towards the pier so dimly lit; there the launch awaits me, motor already running, the driver of the launch pulls the rope, the launch moves closer, he makes the sign that I understand, I jump on board, and already seated, I start cutting, with this lonely profile, the night's salty humidity; the search, always the search, and these deviations from roads so disconcertingly alien to me; this dry earth where all roads have been erased, and everything had been so easy in the 17th Century when I was a woman, hidden in the mystery of the notes of lutes, suffering from impossible loves, that got lost in my long skirts of rich fabrics in that mansion, in the castle, and everything was so easy, to suffer like that, amongst sighs, amongst the notes of the lute, amongst those clothes of rich fabrics and the indoor balcony where we seated ourselves so elegantly reserved, to feel the nervousness of my bosom dispersing through my bulging breasts, and the handkerchief that I gripped in my right hand to calm the desperation of distance, that man in the room next door, who loved me, who did not love me, how impossible our love is, how impossible it could be, but how easy all this was amongst the notes that drip delicately alone, the elegant reserve and the aromatic smoke, the aroma of chapel incense; now my frustration becomes aggressiveness, to pulverize the world with karate chops with the edge of my right hand, because the dislocation becomes intolerable, because the forced march of the search becomes intolerable, and you, Chachi, who share my life in this Twentieth Century in which we can wander without torture the corners of Westchester, you warn me, if you are negative, you will attract that which is negative; at the moment when we set out for the Lyndhurst mansion to drink a strange hot drink, an infusion of fruit and spices, and to listen to the voices of the choir that accompany the flute and the lute, you warn me, that this aggressiveness is my ugly side, and it is alright that you say it like that because this violent corruption is becoming intolerable, and it is alright that the other woman that shared my bed also remembers these moments, the brutal side of me, and she remembers them truthfully, so insistently, until she stretches them to my corners, and you will remember them, woman of now, when you no longer share my bed, and this violent lack of communication will continue being mine, the point of encounter of my atoms sprinkled through the noises of the concrete mixers, through the offices, through the bureaucracy manipulated by the blacks, through the bureaucracy manipulated by the whites, through the tick of the clock that persistently sends me off to a useless task, and there is no-one to shout at, and there is no-one to complain to, and all the nuclei of protest are beginning to burst, and the violent lack of communication stuck to me, accompanying me, reintegrating me, strengthening me in the certainty that no woman will know how to tear it from me with her teeth; and now, when I am almost a man, almost nothing, with my backpack over my shoulder, the noise of the motor, the wet saltiness sticking to my solitary profile, I advance sensing the crack of the wake, in the waters that give way to the force of the prow, and I don't know if I will be able to recognise the town because it wasn't my decision to visit it, because so much time has passed with an incalculable step, and I breathe the salty air deeply so as not to complain about the uncertainty; the running of the motor begins spacing out its noise, heading towards slowness, a gentle shaking, the gentle rocking of the launch against the pier, the tying of the ropes, the foot on the darkened wood, almost soft, and the town, the town appears there, floating in the middle of the darkness, each white house rocking gently in the choppy night sea and I already enter this house with its poorly lit rooms, and in one room, the billiard table, and the militiamen looking at me with an expression of suspicion, looking at each other to communicate something amongst themselves that they will never say to me, and for the first time, I am intimidated by this solitude so full of witnesses, and I follow without questions a militiaman who leads me to the entrance to a hanging bridge, of wood, that will take me to the house next door, and after showing it to me, the militiaman disappears, and I feel the water up to my ankles; I reach the wooden planks, the wooden house, I am about to move onto the yard that I had sensed would be planted with santo domingos, and this large woman, who appears before me, remains standing, drying her wet hands on her apron, looking at me as if she recognizes in me the person who has come to carry out a task that I am not aware of, to fill a destiny I know nothing about, without understanding my surprise, without it occurring to her to explain to me why there is no garden in the yard, only boards, boards that are submerging with my weight so that the water enters to wet my ankles.